SENTIMENT. INC.

Start Publishing PD LLC
Copyright © 2024 by Start Publishing PD LLC

Start Publishing PD is a registered trademark of Start Publishing PD LLC
Manufactured in the United States of America

Cover art: Shutterstock/Taisiya Kozorez

Cover design: Jennifer Do

10 9 8 7 6 5 4 3 2 1

ISBN 979-8-8809-1132-5

SENTIMENT, INC.

by Poul Anderson

The way we feel about another person, or about objects, is often bound up in associations that have no direct connection with the person or object at all. Often, what we call a "change of heart" comes about sheerly from a change in the many associations which make up our present viewpoint. Now, suppose that these associations could be altered artificially, at the option of the person who was in charge of the process....

SHE was twenty-two years old, fresh out of college, full of life and hope, and all set to conquer the world. Colin Fraser happened to be on vacation on Cape Cod, where she was playing summer stock, and went to more shows than he had planned. It wasn't hard to get an introduction, and before long he and Judy Sanders were seeing a lot of each other.

"Of course," she told him one afternoon on the beach, "my real name is Harkness."

He raised his arm, letting the sand run through his fingers. The beach was big and dazzling white around them, the sea galloped in with a steady roar, and a gull rode the breeze overhead. "What was wrong with it?" he asked. "For a professional monicker, I mean."

She laughed and shook the long hair back over her shoulders. "I wanted to live under the name of Sanders," she explained.

"Oh—oh, yes, of course. Winnie the Pooh." He grinned. "Soulmates, that's what we are." It was about then that he decided he'd been a bachelor long enough.

In the fall she went to New York to begin the upward grind—understudy, walk-on parts, shoestring-theaters, and roles in outright turkeys. Fraser returned to Boston for awhile, but his work suffered, he had to keep dashing off to see her.

By spring she was beginning to get places; she had talent and everybody enjoys looking at a brown-eyed blonde. His weekly proposals were also beginning to show some real progress, and he thought that a month or two of steady siege might finish the campaign. So he took leave from his job and went down to New York himself. He'd saved up enough money, and was good enough in his work, to afford it; anyway, he was his own boss—consulting engineer, specializing in mathematical analysis.

He got a furnished room in Brooklyn, and filled in his leisure time—as he thought of it—with some special math courses at Columbia. And he had a lot of friends in town, in a curious variety of professions. Next to Judy, he saw most of the physicist Sworsky, who was an entertaining companion though most of his work was too top-secret even to be mentioned. It was a happy period.

There is always a jarring note, to be sure. In this case, it was the fact that Fraser had plenty of competition. He wasn't good-looking himself—a tall gaunt man of twenty-eight, with a dark hatchet face and perpetually-rumpled clothes. But still, Judy saw more of him than of anyone else, and admitted she was seriously considering his proposal and no other.

He called her up once for a date. "Sorry," she answered. "I'd love to, Colin, but I've already promised tonight. Just so you won't worry, it's Matthew Snyder."

"Hm—the industrialist?"

"Uh-huh. He asked me in such a way it was hard to refuse. But I don't think you have to be jealous, honey. 'Bye now."

Fraser lit his pipe with a certain smugness. Snyder was several times a millionaire, but he was close to sixty, a widower of notably dull conversation. Judy wasn't—Well, no worries, as she'd said. He dropped over to Sworsky's apartment for an evening of chess and bull-shooting.

*

IT WAS early in May, when the world was turning green again, that Judy called Fraser up. "Hi," she said breathlessly. "Busy tonight?"

"Well, I was hoping I'd be, if you get what I mean," he said.

"Look, I want to take you out for a change. Just got some unexpected money and dammit, I want to feel rich for one evening."

"Hmmm—" He scowled into the phone. "I dunno—"

"Oh, get off it, Galahad. I'll meet you in the Dixie lobby at seven. Okay?" She blew him a kiss over the wires, and hung up before he could argue further. He sighed and shrugged. Why not, if she wanted to?

They were in a little Hungarian restaurant, with a couple of Tzigani strolling about playing for them alone, it seemed, when he asked for details. "Did you get a bonus, or what?"

"No." She laughed at him over her drink. "I've turned guinea pig."

"I hope you quit *that* job before we're married!"

"It's a funny deal," she said thoughtfully. "It'd interest you. I've been out a couple of times with this Snyder, you know, and if anything was needed to drive me into your arms, Colin, it's his political lectures."

"Well, bless the Republican Party!" He laid his hand over hers, she didn't withdraw it, but she frowned just a little.

"Colin, you know I want to get somewhere before I marry—see a bit of the world, the theatrical world, before turning hausfrau. Don't be so—Oh, never mind. I like you anyway."

Sipping her drink and setting it down again: "Well, to carry on with the story. I finally gave Comrade Snyder the complete brush-off, and I must say he took it very nicely. But today, this morning, he called asking me to have lunch with him, and I did after he explained. It seems he's got a psychiatrist friend doing research, measuring brain storms or something, and—Do I mean storms? Waves, I guess. Anyway, he wants to measure as many different kinds of people as possible, and Snyder had suggested me. I was supposed to come in for three afternoons running—about two hours each time—and I'd get a hundred dollars per session."

"Hm," said Fraser. "I didn't know psych research was that well-heeled. Who is this mad scientist?"

"His name is Kennedy. Oh, by the way, I'm not supposed to tell anybody; they want to spring it on the world as a surprise or something. But you're different, Colin. I'm excited; I want to talk to somebody about it."

"Sure," he said. "You had a session already?"

"Yes, my first was today. It's a funny place to do research—Kennedy's got a big suite on Fifth Avenue, right up in the classy district. Beautiful office. The name of his outfit is Sentiment, Inc."

"Hm. Why should a research-team take such a name? Well, go on."

"Oh, there isn't much else to tell. Kennedy was very nice. He took me into a laboratory full of all sorts of dials and meters and blinking lights and os—what do you call them? Those things that make wiggly pictures."

"Oscilloscopes. You'll never make a scientist, my dear."

She grinned. "But I know one scientist who'd like to—Never mind! Anyway, he sat me down in a chair and put bands around my wrists and ankles—just like the hot squat—and a big thing like a beauty-parlor hair-drier over my head. Then he fiddled with his dials for awhile, making notes. Then he started saying words at me, and showing me pictures. Some of them were very pretty; some ugly; some funny; some downright horrible.... Anyway, that's all there was to it. After a couple of hours he gave me a check for a hundred dollars and told me to come back tomorrow."

"Hm." Fraser rubbed his chin. "Apparently he was measuring the electric rhythms corresponding to pleasure and dislike. I'd no idea anybody'd made an encephalograph that accurate."

"Well," said Judy, "I've told you why we're celebrating. Now come on, the regular orchestra's tuning up. Let's dance."

They had a rather wonderful evening. Afterward Fraser lay awake for a long time, not wanting to lose a state of happiness in sleep. He considered sleep a hideous waste of time: if he lived to be ninety, he'd have spent almost thirty years unconscious.

*

JUDY was engaged for the next couple of evenings, and Fraser himself was invited to dinner at Sworsky's the night after that. So it wasn't till the end of the week that he called her again.

"Hullo, sweetheart," he said exuberantly. "How's things? I refer to Charles Addams Things, of course."

"Oh—Colin." Her voice was very small, and it trembled.

"Look, I've got two tickets to *H. M. S. Pinafore.* So put on your own pinafore and meet me."

"Colin—I'm sorry, Colin. I can't."

"Huh?" He noticed how odd she sounded, and a leadenness grew within him. "You aren't sick, are you?"

"Colin, I—I'm going to be married."

"*What?*"

"Yes. I'm in love now; really in love. I'll be getting married in a couple of months."

"But—but—"

"I didn't want to hurt you." He heard her begin to cry.

"But who—how—"

"It's Matthew," she gulped. "Matthew Snyder."

He sat quiet for a long while, until she asked if he was still on the line. "Yeah," he said tonelessly. "Yeah, I'm still here, after a fashion." Shaking himself: "Look, I've got to see you. I want to talk to you."

"I can't."

"You sure as hell can," he said harshly.

They met at a quiet little bar which had often been their rendezvous. She watched him with frightened eyes while he ordered martinis.

"All right," he said at last. "What's the story?"

"I—" He could barely hear her. "There isn't any story. I suddenly realized I loved Matt. That's all."

SENTIMENT, INC.

"*Snyder!*" He made it a curse. "Remember what you told me about him before?"

"I felt different then," she whispered. "He's a wonderful man when you get to know him."

And rich. He suppressed the words and the thought. "What's so wonderful specifically?" he asked.

"He—" Briefly, her face was rapt. Fraser had seen her looking at him that way, now and then.

"Go on," he said grimly. "Enumerate Mr. Snyder's good qualities. Make a list. He's courteous, cultured, intelligent, young, handsome, amusing—To hell! *Why,* Judy?"

"I don't know," she said in a high, almost fearful tone. "I just love him, that's all." She reached over the table and stroked his cheek. "I like you a lot, Colin. Find yourself a nice girl and be happy."

His mouth drew into a narrow line. "There's something funny here," he said. "Is it blackmail?"

"No!" She stood up, spilling her drink, and the flare of temper showed him how overwrought she was. "He just happens to be the man I love. That's enough out of you, good-bye, Mr. Fraser."

He sat watching her go. Presently he took up his drink, gulped it barbarously, and called for another.

2

JUAN MARTINEZ had come from Puerto Rico as a boy and made his own way ever since. Fraser had gotten to know him in the army, and they had seen each other from time to time since then. Martinez had gone into the private-eye business and made a good thing of it; Fraser had to get past a very neat-looking receptionist to see him.

"Hi, Colin," said Martinez, shaking hands. He was a small, dark man, with a large nose and beady black eyes that made him resemble a sympathetic mouse. "You look like the very devil."

"I feel that way, too," said Fraser, collapsing into a chair. "You can't go on a three-day drunk without showing it."

"Well, what's the trouble? Cigarette?" Martinez held out a pack. "Girl-friend give you the air?"

"As a matter of fact, yes; that's what I want to see you about."

"This isn't a lonely-hearts club," said Martinez. "And I've told you time and again a private dick isn't a wisecracking superman. Our work is ninety-nine percent routine; and for the other one percent, we call in the police."

"Let me give you the story," said Fraser. He rubbed his eyes wearily as he told it. At the end, he sat staring at the floor.

"Well," said Martinez, "it's too bad and all that. But what the hell, there are other dames. New York has more beautiful women per square inch than any other city except Paris. Latch on to somebody else. Or if you want, I can give you a phone number—"

"You don't understand," said Fraser "I want you to investigate this; I want to know why she did it."

Martinez squinted through a haze of smoke. "Snyder's a rich and powerful man," he said. "Isn't that enough?"

"No," said Fraser, too tired to be angry at the hint. "Judy isn't that kind of a girl. Neither is she the kind to go overboard in a few days, especially when I was there. Sure, that sounds conceited, but dammit, I *know* she cared for me."

"Okay. You suspect pressure was brought to bear?"

"Yeah. It's hard to imagine what. I called up Judy's family in Maine, and they said they were all right, no worries. Nor do I think anything in her own life would give a blackmailer or an extortionist anything to go on. Still—I want to know."

Martinez drummed the desk-top with nervous fingers. "I'll look into it if you insist," he said, "though it'll cost you a pretty penny. Rich men's lives aren't easy to pry into if they've got something they want to hide. But I don't think we'd find out much; your case seems to be only one of a rash of similar ones in the past year."

"Huh?" Fraser looked sharply up.

"Yeah. I follow all the news; and remember the odd facts. There've

11

been a good dozen cases recently, where beautiful young women suddenly married rich men or became their mistresses. It doesn't all get into the papers, but I've got my contacts. I know. In every instance, there was no obvious reason; in fact, the dames seemed very much in love with daddy."

"And the era of the gold-digger is pretty well gone—" Fraser sat staring out the window. It didn't seem right that the sky should be so full of sunshine.

"Well," said Martinez, "you don't need me. You need a psychologist."

Psychologist!

"By God, Juan, I'm going to give you a job anyway!" Fraser leaped to his feet. "You're going to check into an outfit called Sentiment, Inc."

*

A WEEK later, Martinez said, "Yeah, we found it easily enough. It's not in the phone-book, but they've got a big suite right in the high-rent district on Fifth. The address is here, in my written report. Nobody in the building knows much about 'em, except that they're a quiet, well-behaved bunch and call themselves research psychologists. They have a staff of four: a secretary-receptionist; a full-time secretary; and a couple of husky boys who may be bodyguards for the boss. That's this Kennedy, Robert Kennedy. My man couldn't get into his office; the girl said he was too busy and never saw anybody except some regular clients. Nor could he date either of the girls, but he did investigate them.

"The receptionist is just a working girl for routine stuff, married, hardly knows or cares what's going on. The steno is unmarried, has a degree in psych, lives alone, and seems to have no friends except her boss. Who's not her lover, by the way."

"Well, how about Kennedy himself?" asked Fraser.

"I've found out a good bit, but it's all legitimate," said Martinez. "He's about fifty years old, a widower, very steady private life. He's a licensed psychiatrist who used to practice in Chicago, where he also did research in collaboration with a physicist named Gavotti, who's since died. Shortly after that happened—

"No, there's no suspicion of foul play; the physicist was an old man and died of a heart attack. Anyway, Kennedy moved to New York. He still practices, officially, but he doesn't take just anybody; claims that his research only leaves him time for a few." Martinez narrowed his eyes. "The only thing you could hold against him is that he occasionally sees a guy named Bryce, who's in a firm that has some dealings with Amtorg."

"The Russian trading corporation? Hm."

"Oh, that's pretty remote guilt by association, Colin. Amtorg does have legitimate business, you know. We buy manganese from them, among other things. And the rest of Kennedy's connections are all strictly blue ribbon. *Crème de la crème*—business, finance, politics, and one big union-leader who's known to be a conservative. In fact, Kennedy's friends are so powerful you'd have real trouble doing anything against him."

Fraser slumped in his chair. "I suppose my notion was pretty wild," he admitted.

"Well, there is one queer angle. You know these rich guys who've suddenly made out with such highly desirable dames? As far as I could find out, every one of them is a client of Kennedy's."

"Eh?" Fraser jerked erect.

"'S a fact. Also, my man showed the building staff, elevator pilots and so on, pictures of these women, and a couple of 'em were remembered as having come to see Kennedy."

"Shortly before they—fell in love?"

"Well, that I can't be sure of. You know how people are about remembering dates. But it's possible."

Fraser shook his dark head. "It's unbelievable," he said. "I thought Svengali was outworn melodrama."

SENTIMENT, INC.

"I know something about hypnotism, Colin. It won't do anything like what you think happened to those girls."

Fraser got out his pipe and fumbled tobacco into it. "I think," he said, "I'm going to call on Dr. Robert Kennedy myself."

"Take it easy, boy," said Martinez. "You been reading too many weird stories; you'll just get tossed out on your can."

Fraser tried to smile. It was hard—Judy wouldn't answer his calls and letters any more. "Well," he said, "it'll be in a worthy cause."

*

THE elevator let him out on the nineteenth floor. It held four big suites, with the corridor running between them. He studied the frosted-glass doors. On one side was the Eagle Publishing Company and Frank & Dayles, Brokers. On the other was the Messenger Advertising Service, and Sentiment, Inc. He entered their door and stood in a quiet, oak-paneled reception room. Behind the railing were a couple of desks, a young woman working at each, and two burly men who sat boredly reading magazines.

The pretty girl, obviously the receptionist, looked up as Fraser approached and gave him a professional smile. "Yes, sir?" she asked.

"I'd like to see Dr. Kennedy, please," he said, trying hard to be casual.

"Do you have an appointment, sir?"

"No, but it's urgent."

"I'm sorry, sir; Dr. Kennedy is very busy. He can't see anybody except his regular patients and research subjects."

"Look, take him in this note, will you? Thanks."

Fraser sat uneasily for some minutes, wondering if he'd worded the note correctly. *I must see you about Miss Judy Harkness. Important.* Well, what the devil else could you say?

The receptionist came out again. "Dr. Kennedy can spare you a few minutes, sir," she said. "Go right on in."

"Thanks." Fraser slouched toward the inner door. The two men lowered their magazines to follow him with watchful eyes.

14

There was a big, handsomely-furnished office inside, with a door beyond that must lead to the laboratory. Kennedy looked up from some papers and rose, holding out his hand. He was a medium-sized man, rather plump, graying hair brushed thickly back from a broad, heavy face behind rimless glasses. "Yes?" His voice was low and pleasant. "What can I do for you?"

"My name's Fraser." The visitor sat down and accepted a cigarette. Best to act urbanely. "I know Miss Harkness well. I understand you made some encephalographic studies of her."

"Indeed?" Kennedy looked annoyed, and Fraser recalled that Judy had been asked not to tell anyone. "I'm not sure; I would have to consult my records first." He wasn't admitting anything, thought Fraser.

"Look," said the engineer, "there's been a marked change in Miss Harkness recently. I know enough psychology to be certain that such changes don't happen overnight without cause. I wanted to consult you."

"I'm not her psychiatrist," said Kennedy coldly. "Now if you will excuse me, I really have a lot to do—"

"All right," said Fraser. There was no menace in his tones, only a weariness. "If you insist, I'll play it dirty. Such abrupt changes indicate mental instability. But I know she was perfectly sane before. It begins to look as if your experiments may have—injured her mind. If so, I should have to report you for malpractice."

Kennedy flushed. "I am a licensed psychiatrist," he said, "and any other doctor will confirm that Miss Harkness is still in mental health. If you tried to get an investigation started, you would only be wasting your own time and that of the authorities. She herself will testify that no harm was done to her; no compulsion applied; and that you are an infernal busybody with some delusions of your own. Good afternoon."

"Ah," said Fraser, "so she *was* here."

Kennedy pushed a button. His men entered. "Show this gentleman the way out, please," he said.

Fraser debated whether to put up a fight, decided it was futile, and went out between the two others. When he got to the street, he found he was shaking, and badly in need of a drink.

*

FRASER asked, "Jim, did you ever read *Trilby?*"

Sworsky's round, freckled face lifted to regard him. "Years ago," he answered. "What of it?"

"Tell me something. Is it possible—even theoretically possible—to do what Svengali did? Change emotional attitudes, just like that." Fraser snapped his fingers.

"I don't know," said Sworsky. "Nuclear cross-sections are more in my line. But offhand, I should imagine it might be done ... sometime in the far future. Thought-habits, associational-patterns, the labeling of this as good and that as bad, seem to be matters of established neural paths. If you could selectively alter the polarization of individual neurones—But it's a pretty remote prospect; we hardly know a thing about the brain today."

He studied his friend sympathetically. "I know it's tough to get jilted," he said, "but don't go off your trolley about it."

"I could stand it if someone else had gotten her in the usual kind of way," said Fraser thinly. "But this—Look, let me tell you all I've found out."

Sworsky shook his head at the end of the story. "That's a mighty wild speculation," he murmured. "I'd forget it if I were you."

"Did you know Kennedy's old partner? Gavotti, at Chicago."

"Sure, I met him a few times. Nice old guy, very unworldly, completely wrapped up in his work. He got interested in neurology from the physics angle toward the end of his life, and contributed a lot to cybernetics. What of it?"

"I don't know," said Fraser; "I just don't know. But do me a favor, will you, Jim? Judy won't see me at all, but she knows you and likes you. Ask her to dinner or something. Insist that she come. Then you

16

and your wife find out—whatever you can. Just exactly how she feels about the whole business. What her attitudes are toward everything."

"The name is Sworsky, not Holmes. But sure, I'll do what I can, if you'll promise to try and get rid of this fixation. You ought to see a head-shrinker yourself, you know."

In vino veritas—sometimes too damn much *veritas*.

*

TOWARD the end of the evening, Judy was talking freely, if not quite coherently. "I cared a lot for Colin," she said. "It was pretty wonderful having him around. He's a grand guy. Only Matt—I don't know. Matt hasn't got half of what Colin has; Matt's a single-track mind. I'm afraid I'm just going to be an ornamental convenience to him. Only if you've ever been so you got all dizzy when someone was around, and thought about him all the time he was away—well, that's how he is. Nothing else matters."

"Colin's gotten a funny obsession," said Sworsky cautiously. "He thinks Kennedy hypnotized you for Snyder. I keep telling him it's impossible, but he can't get over the idea."

"Oh, no, no, no," she said with too much fervor. "It's nothing like that. I'll tell you just what happened. We had those two measuring sessions; it was kind of dull but nothing else. And then the third time Kennedy did put me under hypnosis—he called it that, at least. I went to sleep and woke up about an hour later and he sent me home. I felt all good inside, happy, and shlo—slowly I began to see what Matt meant to me.

"I called him up that evening. He said Kennedy's machine *did* speed up people's minds for a short while, sometimes, so they decided quick-like what they'd've worked out anyway. Kennedy is—I don't know. It's funny how ordinary he seemed at first. But when you get to know him, he's like—God, almost. He's strong and wise and good. He—" Her voice trailed off and she sat looking foolishly at her glass.

"You know," said Sworsky, "perhaps Colin is right after all."

"Don't say that!" She jumped up and slapped his face. "Kennedy's *good*, I tell you! All you little lice sitting here making sly remarks behind his back, and he's so, much bigger than all of you and—" She broke into tears and stormed out of the apartment.

Sworsky reported the affair to Fraser. "I wonder," he said. "It doesn't seem natural, I'll agree. But what can anybody do? The police?"

"I've tried," said Fraser dully. "They laughed. When I insisted, I damn near got myself jugged. That's no use. The trouble is, none of the people who've been under the machine will testify against Kennedy. He fixes it so they worship him."

"I still think you're crazy. There *must* be a simpler hypothesis; I refuse to believe your screwy notions without some real evidence. But what are you going to do now?"

"Well," said Fraser with a tautness in his voice, "I've got several thousand dollars saved up, and Juan Martinez will help. Ever hear the fable about the lion? He licked hell out of the bear and the tiger and the rhinoceros, but a little gnat finally drove him nuts. Maybe I can be the gnat." He shook his head. "But I'll have to hurry. The wedding's only six weeks off."

3

IT CAN be annoying to be constantly shadowed; to have nasty gossip about you spreading through the places where you work and live; to find your tires slashed; to be accosted by truculent drunks when you stop in for a quick one; to have loud horns blow under your window every night. And it doesn't do much good to call the police; your petty tormentors always fade out of sight.

Fraser was sitting in his room some two weeks later, trying unsuccessfully to concentrate on matrix algebra, when the phone rang. He never picked it up without a fluttering small hope that it might be Judy, and it never was. This time it was a man's voice: "Mr. Fraser?"

"Yeah," he grunted. "Wha'dya want?"

"This is Robert Kennedy. I'd like to talk to you."

Fraser's heart sprang in his ribs, but he held his voice stiff. "Go on, then. Talk."

"I want you to come up to my place. We may be having a long conversation."

"Mmmm—well—" It was more than he had allowed himself to hope for, but he remained curt: "Okay. But a full report of this business, and what I think you're doing, is in the hands of several people. If anything should happen to me—"

"You've been reading too many hard-boileds," said Kennedy. "Nothing will happen. Anyway, I have a pretty good idea who those people are; I can hire detectives of my own, you know."

"I'll come over, then." Fraser hung up and realized, suddenly, that he was sweating.

The night air was cool as he walked down the street. He paused for a moment, feeling the city like a huge impersonal machine around him, grinding and grinding. Human civilization had grown too big, he thought. It was beyond anyone's control; it had taken on a will of its own and was carrying a race which could no longer guide it. Sometimes—reading the papers, or listening to the radio, or just watching the traffic go by like a river of steel—a man could feel horribly helpless.

He took the subway to Kennedy's address, a swank apartment in the lower Fifties. He was admitted by the psychiatrist in person; no one else was around.

"I assume," said Kennedy, "that you don't have some wild idea of pulling a gun on me. That would accomplish nothing except to get you in trouble."

"No," said Fraser, "I'll be good." His eyes wandered about the living room. One wall was covered with books which looked used; there were some quality reproductions, a Capehart, and fine, massive furniture. It was a tasteful layout. He looked a little more closely at three pictures on the mantel: a middle-aged woman and two young men in uniform.

"My wife," said Kennedy, "and my boys. They're all dead. Would you like a drink?"

"No. I came to talk."

"I'm not Satan, you know," said Kennedy. "I like books and music, good wine, good conversation. I'm as human as you are, only I have a purpose."

Fraser sat down and began charging his pipe. "Go ahead," he said. "I'm listening."

Kennedy pulled a chair over to face him. The big smooth countenance behind the rimless glasses held little expression. "Why have you been annoying me?" he asked.

"I?" Fraser lifted his brows.

Kennedy made an impatient gesture. "Let's not chop words. There are no witnesses tonight. I intend to talk freely, and want you to do the same. I know that you've got Martinez sufficiently convinced to help you with this very childish persecution-campaign. What do you hope to get out of it?"

"I want my girl back," said Fraser tonelessly. "I was hoping my nuisance-value—"

*

KENNEDY winced a bit. "You know, I'm damned sorry about that. It's the one aspect of my work which I hate. I'd like you to believe that I'm not just a scientific procurer. Actually, I have to satisfy the minor desires of my clients, so they'll stay happy and agree to my major wishes. It's the plain truth that those women have been only the minutest fraction of my job."

"Nevertheless, you're a free-wheeling son, doing something like that—"

"Really, now, what's so horrible about it? Those girls are in love—the normal, genuine article. It's not any kind of zombie state, or whatever your overheated imagination has thought up. They're entirely sane, unharmed, and happy. In fact, happiness of that kind is so rare in this world that if I wanted to, I could pose as their benefactor."

"You've got a machine," said Fraser; "it changes the mind. As far as I'm concerned, that's as gross a violation of liberty as throwing somebody into a concentration camp."

"How free do you think anyone is? You're born with a fixed heredity. Environment molds you like clay. Your society teaches you what and how to think. A million tiny factors, all depending on blind, uncontrollable chance, determine the course of your life—including your love-life.... Well, we needn't waste any time on philosophy. Go on, ask some questions. I admit I've hurt you—unwittingly, to be sure—but I do want to make amends."

"Your machine, then," said Fraser. "How did you get it? How does it work."

"I was practicing in Chicago," said Kennedy, "and collaborating on the side with Gavotti. How much do you know of cybernetics? I don't mean computers and automata, which are only one aspect of the field; I mean control and communication, in the animal as well as in the machine."

"Well, I've read Wiener's books, and studied Shannon's work, too." Despite himself, Fraser was thawing, just a trifle. "It's exciting stuff. Communications-theory seems to be basic, in biology and psychology as well as in electronics."

"Quite. The future may remember Wiener as the Galileo of neurology. If Gavotti's work ever gets published, he'll be considered the Newton. So far, frankly, I've suppressed it. He died suddenly, just when his machine was completed and he was getting ready to publish his results. Nobody but I knew anything more than rumors; he was inclined to be secretive till he had a *fait accompli* on hand. I realized what an opportunity had been given me, and took it; I brought the machine here without saying much to anyone."

Kennedy leaned back in his chair. "I imagine it was mostly luck which took Gavotti and me so far," he went on. "We made a long series of improbably good guesses, and thus telescoped a century of work into a decade. If I were religious, I'd be down on my knees, thanking the Lord for putting this thing of the future into my hands."

"Or the devil," said Fraser.

Briefly, anger flitted across Kennedy's face. "I grant you, the machine is a terrible power, but it's harmless to a man if it's used properly—as I have used it. I'm not going to tell you just how it works; to be perfectly honest, I only understand a fraction of its theory and its circuits myself. But look, you know something of encephalography. The various basic rhythms of the brain have been measured. The standard method is already so sensitive that it can detect abnormalities like a developing tumor or a strong emotional disturbance, that will give trouble unless corrected. Half of Gavotti's machine is a still more delicate encephalograph. It can measure and analyze the minute variations in electrical pulses corresponding to the basic emotional states. It won't read thoughts, no; but once calibrated for a given individual, it will tell you if he's happy, sorrowful, angry, disgusted, afraid—any fundamental neuro-glandular condition, or any combination of them."

He paused. "All right," said Fraser. "What else does it do?"

"It does *not* make monsters," said Kennedy. "Look, the specific emotional reaction to a given stimulus is, in the normal individual, largely a matter of conditioned reflex, instilled by social environment or the accidental associations of his life.

"Anyone in decent health will experience fear in the presence of danger; desire in the presence of a sexual object, and so on. That's basic biology, and the machine can't change that. But most of our evaluations are learned. For instance, to an American the word 'mother' has powerful emotional connotations, while to a Samoan it means nothing very exciting. You had to develop a taste for liquor, tobacco, coffee—in fact most of what you consume. If you're in love with a particular woman, it's a focusing of the general sexual libido on her, brought about by the symbolizing part of your mind: she *means* something to you. There are cultures without romantic love, you know. And so on. All these specific, conditioned reactions can be changed."

"How?"

*

KENNEDY thought for a moment "The encephalographic part of the machine measures the exact pulsations in the individual corresponding to the various emotional reactions. It takes me about four hours to determine those with the necessary precision; then I have to make statistical analyses of the data, to winnow out random variations. Thereafter I put the subject in a state of light hypnosis—that's only to increase suggestibility, and make the process faster. As I pronounce the words and names I'm interested in, the machine feeds back the impulses corresponding to the emotions I want: a sharply-focused beam on the brain center concerned.

"For instance, suppose you were an alcoholic and I wanted to cure you. I'd put you in hypnosis and stand there whispering 'wine, whisky, beer, gin,' and so on; meanwhile, the machine would be feeding the impulses corresponding to your reactions of hate, fear, and disgust into your brain. You'd come out unchanged, except that your appetite for alcohol would be gone; you could, in fact, come out hating the stuff so much that you'd join the Prohibition Party—though, in actual practice, it would probably be enough just to give you a mild aversion."

"Mmmm—I see. Maybe." Fraser scowled. "And the—subject—doesn't remember what you've done?"

"Oh, no. It all takes place on the lower subconscious levels. A new set of conditioned neural pathways is opened, you see, and old ones are closed off. The brain does that by itself, through its normal symbolizing mechanism. All that happens is that the given symbol—such as liquor—becomes reflectively associated with the given emotional state, such as dislike."

SENTIMENT. INC.

Kennedy leaned forward with an air of urgency. "The end result is in no way different from ordinary means of persuasion. Propaganda does the same thing by sheer repetition. If you're courting a girl, you try to identify yourself in her mind with the things she desires, by appropriate behavior.... I'm sorry; I shouldn't have used that example.... The machine is only a direct, fast way of doing this, producing a more stable result."

"It's still—tampering," said Fraser. "How do you know you're not creating side-effects, doing irreparable long-range damage?"

"Oh, for Lord's sake!" exploded Kennedy. "Take your mind off that shelf, will you? I've told you how delicate the whole thing is. A few microwatts of power more or less, a frequency-shift of less than one percent, and it doesn't work at all. There's no effect whatsoever." He cooled off fast, adding reflectively: "On the given subject, that is. It might work on someone else. These pulsations are a highly individual matter; I have to calibrate every case separately."

There was a long period of silence. Then Fraser strained forward and said in an ugly voice:

"All right You've told me how you do it. Now tell me *why*. What possible reason or excuse, other than your own desire to play God? This thing could be the greatest psychiatric tool in history, and you're using it to—pimp!"

"I told you that was unimportant," said Kennedy quietly. "I'm doing much more. I set up in practice here in New York a couple of years ago. Once I had a few chance people under control—no, I tell you again, I didn't make robots of them. I merely associated myself, in their own minds, with the father-image. That's something I do to everyone who comes under the machine, just as a precaution if nothing else, Kennedy is all-wise, all-powerful; Kennedy can do no wrong. It isn't a conscious realization; to the waking mind, I am only a shrewd adviser and a damn swell fellow. But the subconscious mind knows otherwise. It wouldn't *let* my subjects act against me; it wouldn't even let them want to.

24

"Well, you see how it goes. I got those first few people to recommend me to certain selected friends, and these in turn recommended me to others. Not necessarily as a psychiatrist; I have variously been a doctor, a counsellor, or merely a research-man looking for data. But I'm building up a group of the people I want. People who'll back me up, who'll follow my advice—not with any knowledge of being dominated, but because the workings of their own subconscious minds will lead them inevitably to think that my advice is the only sound policy to follow and my requests are things any decent man must grant."

"Yeah," said Fraser. "I get it. Big businessmen. Labor-leaders. Politicians. Military men. And Soviet spies!"

*

KENNEDY nodded. "I have connections with the Soviets; their agents think I'm on their side. But it isn't treason, though I may help them out from time to time.

"That's why I have to do these services for my important clients, such as getting them the women they want—or, what I actually do more often, influencing their competitors and associates. You see, the subconscious mind knows I am all-powerful, but the conscious mind doesn't. It has to be satisfied by occasional proofs that I *am* invaluable; otherwise conflicts would set in, my men would become unstable and eventually psychotic, and be of no further use to me.

"Of course," he added, almost pedantically, "my men don't know how I persuade these other people—they only know that I do, somehow, and their regard for their own egos, as well as for me, sets up a bloc which prevents them from reasoning out the fact that they themselves are dominated. They're quite content to accept the results of my help, without inquiring further into the means than the easy rationalization that I have a 'persuasive personality.'

"I don't like what I'm doing, Fraser. But it's got to be done."

"You still haven't said *what's* got to be done," answered the engineer coldly.

25

SENTIMENT, INC.

"I've been given something unbelievable," said Kennedy. His voice was very soft now. "If I'd made it public, can you imagine what would have happened? Psychiatrists would use it, yes; but so would criminals, dictators, power-hungry men of all kinds. Even in this country, I don't think libertarian principles could long survive. It would be too simple—

"And yet it would have been cowardly to break the machine and burn Gavotti's notes. Chance has given me the power to be more than a chip in the river—a river that's rapidly approaching a waterfall, war, destruction, tyranny, no matter who the Pyrrhic victor may be. I'm in a position to do something for the causes in which I believe."

"And what are they?" asked Fraser.

Kennedy gestured at the pictures on the mantel. "Both my sons were killed in the last war. My wife died of cancer—a disease which would be licked now if a fraction of the money spent on armaments had been diverted to research. That brought it home to me; but there are hundreds of millions of people in worse cases. And war isn't the only evil—there is poverty, oppression, inequality, want and suffering. It could be changed.

"I'm building up my own lobby, you might say. In a few more years, I hope to be the indispensable adviser of all the men who, between them, really run this country. And yes, I have been in touch with Soviet agents—have even acted as a transmitter of stolen information. The basic problem of spying, you know, is not to get the information in the first place as much as to get it to the homeland. Treason? No. I think not. I'm getting my toehold in world communism. I already have some of its agents; sooner or later, I'll get to the men who really matter. Then communism will no longer be a menace."

He sighed. "It's a hard row to hoe. It'll take my lifetime, at least; but what else have I got to give my life to?"

Fraser sat quiet. His pipe was cold, he knocked it out and began filling it afresh. The scratching of his match seemed unnaturally loud. "It's too much," he said. "It's too big a job for one man to tackle. The world will stumble along somehow, but you'll just get things into a worse mess."

"I've got to try," said Kennedy.

"And I still want my girl back."

"I can't do that; I need Snyder too much. But I'll make it up to you somehow." Kennedy sighed. "Lord, if you knew how much I've wanted to tell all this!"

With sudden wariness: "Not that it's to be repeated. In fact, you're to lay off me; call off your dogs. Don't try to tell anyone else what I've told you. You'd never be believed and I already have enough power to suppress the story, if you should get it out somehow. And if you give me any more trouble at all, I'll see to it that you—stop."

"Murder?"

"Or commitment to an asylum. I can arrange that too."

Fraser sighed. He felt oddly unexcited, empty, as if the interview had drained him of his last will to resist. He held the pipe loosely in his fingers, letting it go out.

"Ask me a favor," urged Kennedy. "I'll do it, if it won't harm my own program. I tell you, I want to square things."

"Well—"

"Think about it. Let me know."

"All right." Fraser got up. "I may do that." He went out the door without saying goodnight.

4

HE sat with his feet on the table, chair tilted back and teetering dangerously, hands clasped behind his head, pipe filling the room with blue fog. It was his usual posture for attacking a problem.

And damn it, he thought wearily, this was a question such as he made his living on. An industrial engineer comes into the office. We want this and that—a machine for a very special purpose, let's say.

SENTIMENT. INC.

What should we do, Mr. Fraser? Fraser prowls around the plant, reads up on the industry, and then sits down and thinks. The elements of the problem are such-and-such; how can they be combined to yield a solution?

Normally, he uses the mathematical approach, especially in machine design. Most practicing-engineers have a pathetic math background—they use ten pages of elaborate algebra and rusty calculus to figure out something that three vector equations would solve. But you have to get the logical basics straight first, before you can set up your equations.

All right, what is the problem? To get Judy back. That means forcing Kennedy to restore her normal emotional reactions—no, he didn't want her thrust into love of him; he just wanted her as she had been.

What are the elements of the problem? Kennedy acts outside the law, but he has blocked all official channels. He even has connections extending through the Iron Curtain.

Hmmmm—appeal to the FBI? Kennedy couldn't have control over them—*yet*. However, if Fraser tried to tip off the FBI, they'd act cautiously, if they investigated at all. They'd have to go slow. And Kennedy would find out in time to do something about it.

Martinez could help no further. Sworsky had closer contact with Washington. He'd been so thoroughly cleared that they'd be inclined to trust whatever he said. But Sworsky doubted the whole story; like many men who'd suffered through irresponsible Congressional charges, he was almost fanatic about having proof before accusing anyone of anything. Moreover, Kennedy knew that Sworsky was Fraser's friend; he'd probably be keeping close tabs on the physicist and ready to block any attempts he might make to help. With the backing of a man like Snyder, Kennedy could hire as many detectives as he wanted.

In fact, whatever the counter-attack, it was necessary to go warily. Kennedy's threat to get rid of Fraser if the engineer kept working against him was not idle mouthing. He could do it—and, being a fanatic, would.

But Kennedy, like the demon of legend, would grant one wish—just to salve his own conscience. Only what should the wish be? Another woman? Or merely to be reconciled, artificially, to an otherwise-intolerable situation?

Judy, Judy, Judy!

Fraser swore at himself. Damn it to hell, this was a problem in logic. No room for emotion. Of course, it might be a problem without a solution. There are plenty of those.

He squinted, trying to visualize the office. He thought of burglary, stealing evidence—silly thought. But let's see, now. What was the layout, exactly? Four suites on one floor of the skyscraper, three of them unimportant offices of unimportant men. And—

Oh, Lord!

Fraser sat for a long while, hardly moving. Then he uncoiled himself and ran, downstairs and into the street and to the nearest pay phone. His own line might be tapped—

"Hello, hello, Juan?... Yes, I know I got you out of bed, and I'm not sorry. This is too bloody important.... Okay, okay.... Look, I want a complete report on the Messenger Advertising Service.... When? Immediately, if not sooner. And I mean *complete*.... That's right, Messenger.... Okay, fine. I'll buy you a drink sometime."

"Hello, Jim? Were you asleep too?... Sorry.... But look, would you make a list of all the important men you know fairly well? I need it bad.... No, don't come over. I think I'd better not see you for a while. Just mail it to me.... All right, so I am paranoid...."

*

JEROME K. FERRIS was a large man, with a sense of his own importance that was even larger. He sat hunched in the chair, his head dwarfed by the aluminum helmet, his breathing shallow. Around him danced and flickered a hundred meters, indicator lights, tubes. There was a low humming in the room, otherwise it was altogether silent, blocked and shielded against the outside world. The fluorescent lights were a muted glow.

Fraser sat watching the greenish trace on the huge oscilloscope screen. It was an intricate set of convolutions, looking more like a plate of spaghetti than anything else. He wondered how many frequencies were involved. Several thousand, at the very least.

"Fraser," repeated Kennedy softly into the ear of the hypnotized man. "Colin Fraser. Colin Fraser." He touched a dial with infinite care. "Colin Fraser. Colin Fraser."

The oscilloscope flickered as he readjusted, a new trace appeared. Kennedy waited for a while, then: "Robert Kennedy. Sentiment, Inc. Robert Kennedy. Sentiment, Inc. Robert Kennedy. Sentiment—"

He turned off the machine, its murmur and glow died away. Facing Fraser with a tight little smile, he said: "All right. Your job is done. Are we even now?"

"As even, as we'll ever get, I suppose," said Fraser.

"I wish you'd trust me," said Kennedy with a hint of wistfulness. "I'd have done the job honestly; you didn't have to watch."

"Well, I was interested," said Fraser.

"Frankly, I still don't see what you stand to gain by the doglike devotion of this Ferris. He's rich, but he's too weak and short-sighted to be a leader. I'd never planned on conditioning him for my purposes."

"I've explained that," said Fraser patiently. "Ferris is a large stockholder in a number of corporations. His influence can swing a lot of business my way."

"Yes, I know. I didn't grant your wish blindly, you realize. I had Ferris studied; he's unable to harm me." Kennedy regarded Fraser with hard eyes. "And just in case you still have foolish notions, please remember that I gave him the father-conditioning with respect to myself. He'll do a lot for you, but not if it's going to hurt me in any way."

"I know when I'm licked," said Fraser bleakly; "I'm getting out of town as soon as I finish those courses I'm signed up for."

Kennedy snapped his fingers. "All right, Ferris, wake up now."

Ferris blinked. "What's been happening?" he asked.

"Nothing much," said Kennedy, unbuckling the electrodes. "I've taken my readings. Thank you very much for the help, sir. I'll see that you get due credit when my research is published."

"Ah—yes. Yes." Ferris puffed himself out. Then he put an arm around Fraser's shoulder. "If you aren't busy," he said, "maybe we could go have lunch."

"Thanks," said Fraser. "I'd like to talk to you about a few things."

He lingered for a moment after Ferris had left the room. "I imagine this is goodbye for us," he said.

"Well, so long, at least. We'll probably hear from each other again." Kennedy shook Fraser's hand. "No hard feelings? I did go to a lot of trouble for you—wangling your introduction to Ferris when you'd named him, and having one of my men persuade him to come here. And right when I'm so infernally busy, too."

"Sure," said Fraser. "It's all right. I can't pretend to love you for what you've done, but you aren't a bad sort."

"No worse than you," said Kennedy with a short laugh. "You've used the machine for your own ends, now."

"Yeah," said Fraser. "I guess I have."

*

SWORSKY asked, "Why do you insist on calling me from drugstores? And why at my office? I've got a home phone, you know."

"I'm not sure but that our own lines are tapped," said Fraser. "Kennedy's a smart cookie, and don't you forget it. I think he's about ready to dismiss me as a danger, but you're certainly being watched; you're on his list."

"You're getting a persecution-complex. Honest, Colin, I'm worried."

"Well, bear with me for a while. Now, have you had any

information on Kennedy since I called last?"

"Hm, no. I did mention to Thomson, as you asked me to, that I'd heard rumors of some revolutionary encephalographic techniques and would be interested in seeing the work. Why did you want me to do that?"

"Thomson," said Fraser, "is one of Kennedy's men. Now look, Jim, before long you're going to be invited to visit Kennedy. He'll give you a spiel about his research and ask to measure your brain waves. I want you to say yes. Then I want to know the exact times of the three appointments he'll give you—the first two, at least."

"Hmmm—if Kennedy's doing what you claim—"

"Jim, it's a necessary risk, but *I'm* the one who's taking it. You'll be okay, I promise you; though perhaps later you'll read of me being found in the river. You see, I got Kennedy to influence a big stockowner for me. One of the lesser companies in which he has a loud voice is Messenger. I don't suppose Kennedy knows that. I hope not!"

*

SWORSKY looked as if he'd been sandbagged. He was white, and the hand that poured a drink shook.

"Lord," he muttered. "Lord, Colin, you were right."

Fraser's teeth drew back from his lips. "You went through with it, eh?"

"Yes. I let the son hypnotize me, and afterward I walked off with a dreamy expression, as you told me to. Just three hours ago, he dropped around here in person. He gave me a long rigmarole about the stupidity of military secrecy, and how the Soviet Union stands for peace and justice. I hope I acted impressed; I'm not much of an actor."

"You don't have to be. Just so you didn't overdo it. To one of Kennedy's victims, obeying his advice is so natural that it doesn't call for any awe-struck wonderment."

"And he wanted data from me! Bombardment cross-sections.

Critical values. Resonance levels. My Lord, if the Russians found that out through spies it'd save them three years of research. This is an FBI case, all right."

"No, not yet." Fraser laid an urgent hand on Sworsky's arm. "You've stuck by me so far, Jim. Go along a little further."

"What do you want me to do?"

"Why—" Fraser's laugh jarred out. "Give him what he wants, of course."

*

KENNEDY looked up from his desk, scowling. "All right, Fraser," he said. "You've been a damned nuisance, and it's pretty patient of me to see you again. But this is the last time. Wha'd'you want?"

"It's the last time I'll need to see you, perhaps." Fraser didn't sit down. He stood facing Kennedy. "You've had it, friend; straight up."

"What do you mean?" Kennedy's hand moved toward his buzzer.

"Listen before you do anything," said Fraser harshly. "I know you tried to bring Jim Sworsky under the influence. You asked him for top-secret data. A few hours ago, you handed the file he brought you on to Bryce, who's no doubt at the Amtorg offices this minute. That's high treason, Kennedy; they execute people for doing that."

The psychologist slumped back.

"Don't try to have your bully boys get rid of me," said Fraser. "Sworsky is sitting by the phone, waiting to call the FBI. I'm the only guy who can stop him."

"But—" Kennedy's tongue ran around his lips. "But he committed treason himself. He gave me the papers!"

Fraser grinned. "You don't think those were authentic, do you? I doubt if you'll be very popular in the Soviet Union either, once they've tried to build machines using your data."

Kennedy looked down at the floor. "How did you do it?" he whispered.

"Remember Ferris? The guy you fixed up for me? He owns a share of your next-door neighbor, the Messenger Advertising Service. I fed him a song and dance about needing an office to do some important work, only my very whereabouts had to be secret. The Messenger people were moved out without anybody's knowing. I installed myself there one night, also a simple little electric oscillator.

"Encephalography is damn delicate work; it involves amplifications up to several million. The apparatus misbehaves if you give it a hard look. Naturally, your lab and the machine were heavily shielded, but even so, a radio emitter next door would be bound to throw you off. My main trouble was in lousing you up just a little bit, not enough to make you suspect anything.

"I only worked at that during your calibrating sessions with Sworsky. I didn't have to be there when you turned the beam on him, because it would be calculated from false data and be so far from his pattern as to have no effect. You told me yourself how precise an adjustment was needed. Sworsky played along, then. Now we've got proof—not that you meddled with human lives, but that you are a spy."

Kennedy sat without moving. His voice was a broken mumble. "I was going to change the world. I had hopes for all humankind. And you, for the sake of one woman—"

"I never trusted anybody with a messiah complex. The world is too big to change single-handed; you'd just have bungled it up worse than it already is. A lot of dictators started out as reformers and ended up as mass-executioners; you'd have done the same."

Fraser leaned over his desk. "I'm willing to make a deal, though," he went on. "Your teeth are pulled; there's no point in turning you in. Sworsky and Martinez and I are willing just to report on Bryce, and let you go, if you'll change back all your subjects. We're going to read your files, and watch and see that you do it. Every one."

Kennedy bit his lip. "And the machine—?"

"I don't know. We'll settle that later. Okay, God, here's the phone number of Judy Harkness. Ask her to come over for a special treatment. At once."

34

POUL ANDERSON

*

A MONTH later, the papers had a story about a plausible maniac who had talked his way into the Columbia University laboratories, where Gavotti's puzzling machine was being studied, and pulled out a hammer and smashed it into ruin before he could be stopped. Taken to jail, he committed suicide in his cell. The name was Kennedy.

Fraser felt vague regret, but it didn't take him long to forget it; he was too busy making plans for his wedding.